Femdom Wife Takes Control:

The Full Trilogy

By Jon Zelig

Get a FREE eBook!

Write a Review: Just review anything by Jon, Joy, Zoë or Bram Zelig, post to Amazon, Goodreads, or another book review site or blog, and send me a link and your email address.

OR

Sign up for our Email List:

http://eepurl.com/cKUGov

jonzelig@protonmail.com

Disclaimers

- Readers offended by the explicit description of sexual acts, as well as all those under the age of eighteen—or the "adult content" age threshold under the laws of their own countries or jurisdictions—should not continue reading.
- This story is an explicit and sexually graphic depiction of *power exchange* relationships between characters who are all consenting adults.
- This is *not* a representation of non-consensual sexual practices, which the author does not in any way endorse or condone.
- This is a work of fiction: Any resemblance to real persons, living or dead, is purely coincidental.

The Zelig Family

Weird genetics? Something in the water? Odd family dynamics? Whatever it is . . . The Zeligs *do* seem to be a little . . . erotically obsessed. But each one in their own particular way:

Bram Zelig skews toward Paranormal Romance & Erotica.

Jon Zelig does Femdom, often w/ elements of age play, cuckolding & male chastity.

Joy Zelig—Jon's twin and mirror image—does more Maledom.

Zoë Zelig is softer; BDSM, Maledom oriented, but more romantic, something of a *Fifty Shades of Grey*-inflected focus on wealth & power.

Their characters tend to love one another and they have an ongoing interest in the moral underpinnings of power exchange: What's consent, where are the lines, who gets to judge—sexually or emotionally? What's public and what's private? When do pain and pleasure shade into damage?

They're trying to do what we all try to do: just . . . make it work.

www.amazon.com/author/bramzelig
www.amazon.com/author/jonzelig
www.amazon.com/author/joyzelig
www.amazon.com/author/zoezelig

Author's Note

The work contained in this volume was originally published as three separate but linked vignettes which, for the most part, are no longer available on line.

Some artifacts of formatting—like sub-titling this as a "trilogy" and naming the main sections "books"—are remnants of that publishing history. In a few cases the second and third sections repeat some information from the first—which was meant to "catch up" people who had not read that first "book."

Apologies for any confusion this may cause.

Table of Contents

Book I: You Put a Chip Where!?

Book II: Teaching Lessons & Learning Rules

Book III: Too Far?

BONUS Chapter!

Femdom Wife Takes Control
Book I: You Put a Chip *Where!?*

Chipping In

Yes: I enjoyed watching my husband "come out of it," post-surgically.

Yes: Because I wanted to catch that exact "moment of realization."

Yes: Because I'd had them do a *little* more than just cutting the melanoma off his calf.

And . . . Yes: I'd had him *Dick-Chipped.*

Best $5000 I ever spent!

Had to have a veterinarian do it—"real docs" had *issues?*

Concerns me not at all: I recommend it highly.

I was sweet and loving—my specialty!—as he woke up, stroking his hair, looking affectionately into his eyes as they opened, flickered, finally focused.

Then I waited for a very particular *kind* of blink.

A little bit of puzzlement.

A little bit of pain.

And a little bit of . . . panic.

The sudden recognition of a sting where he didn't expect to feel it—different from the whole "regaining consciousness and getting oriented" series of blinks.

Those are a whole other thing; you understand what I mean or you don't.

If you're lucky—or if you're a woman with a husband, and you have half a brain—you'll understand in the near to medium term future.

"Hey," I said softly, as he re-surfaced. "Leg doesn't hurt too much?"

Well—of course it didn't!—not yet.

They'd numbed him up pretty good after they put him out.

But that heat and sting on the underside of his cock, just below the corona?

Wouldn't take more than a quick minute—I had been, quite accurately, assured—for that to come into sharp focus.

Took maybe "a minute-twenty."

I didn't clock it or—*not quite*—count it off.

But . . . it was definitely under ninety seconds.

And watching his little "face ballet," before he was *ready to share?*

That was fascinating—and *highly* entertaining!—as well.

I'm sure the sedation helped—a little i.v. cocktail can be more effective than a scotch or two.

"*Why* do I—?" he began, first looking directly at me, then looking away.

Eyes steady, I gave a little, encouraging and curious, hum.

What could he *possibly* be concerned about?

I don't bother much with wide-eyed innocence.

Why should I?

It's silly and tiresome.

But in this case?

Well . . .

He looked back at me.

In that brief but *gorgeous* confusion.

And then . . ?

I watched that *beautiful* cascade.

A twinge of pain.

A flash of upset.

A very quick moment of something like analysis.

And then?

That *Slam!* of realization.

"What did you *do?*" he asked hoarsely, eyes suddenly— *wonderfully!*—fearful.

Really?

Just . . . *panty-dampeningly-fearful.*

It's not that I want to crush him.

Not . . . exactly.

2

After all, I—*don't-ask-me-why* but—I want to stay married to him.

But—in, brief, honest moments, he'd say this himself—he's been out of control.

He's been *in need of help.*

For some time now.

"I *helped* you," I said, with what he might have heard as ominous reassurance.

"*How* . . ?" he asked carefully.

My pause *was* to . . . torture him.

Just a little.

Just . . . *a little.*

"There's maybe some . . . *sting-and-burn*, just a *little* south of *Mr. Happy's Head?*" I asked, more light and interested than in any way severe.

"What. Did. You. *Do?*" he asked again, more tremulous than harsh, close to a plea, which was a good call on his part.

Him talking to *me* harshly?

Among *so* many other varieties of disrespect?

That was now in his rearview mirror—and would be receding fast.

Very.

Fast.

"Torturing" him—really more psychically than physically?

That would come later.

In-the-moment?

Just being direct felt like the right way to go.

"I had you *Dick-Chipped.*"

He simply closed his eyes and moaned.

Just a . . . *panty-dampening* moan.

Oh, *yes!*

"And . . . *now?*" he whispered.

Nice shift to "the practical."

I appreciated that.

And it was a good move on his part.

Well, like I said: I do want to keep him; I've always thought him . . . *educable.*

Plus, now more than ever, perhaps he understands: *Resistance is Futile.*

Recognizing reality is an important first step, *accepting* it a close and crucial second.

Felt like we were well on our way—there being, of course, further steps down . . .

I fished my phone out of my purse, but merely held it where we both could see it.

I gently kissed his cheek, softly flicked his earlobe with my tongue, considered biting but held off, then drew back only slightly.

"You get *hard?*" I purred, waving my phone vaguely in his direction. "I'll see it."

He closed his eyes in acknowledgment.

"You get a little . . . *Rubby-with-your-Chubby?* I'll see that, too."

Eyes still closed, he nodded hurriedly.

"*And,*" I said, trying not at all to keep a measure of anger from my voice, "if you are *fucking? Look!*" I hissed, waving the phone in front of his face and waiting until he opened his eyes again and focused, "and you are not fucking *the-only-person-you-should-ever-fuck-again?*" I paused only briefly. "I *will.* See. It," I bit off.

"*And,*" I flicked a finger on his forehead, making him wince—and pay attention—showing him the app on my screen, "do you see that red button?"

He got a little whiney—shading toward surly.

That was fine.

Bring it to the surface, so I can train it out, I thought; it was more than time.

"Do you *see.* The button?" I repeated. "*Use your words,*" I coaxed.

Yes: He *is* a toddler.

He closed his eyes again as he nodded, expression pained.

4

I let that go.

I leaned in, kissed him again, reached down and cupped his cock under the hospital gown that was still all that he wore—gently: I knew he was sore.

After all: I'd *paid* to make him sore.

I whispered in his ear, as though sharing a happy secret: "Do you want to know what the button does?"

It wasn't quite a sob; it was close.

"*No.*"

Credit again for honesty?

"Well . . . Okay, then. You don't have to look. I'll just *Show & Tell*—" I felt him tense, which was wholly appropriate, "—you how it works."

I didn't give him time to plead or protest.

Just shocked him.

Briefly.

And at a *very* low level—the lowest possible, really—first putting a hand firmly over his mouth.

After all: Not a good thing for other people on the Post-Op Ward to hear screaming.

Mostly, I was able to smother his cry.

Mostly.

I held and soothed him for a quick minute.

In the aftermath.

"It's *okay*," I whispered, cradling him as he trembled and cried. "It's okay. *It is.* Or . . . it will be. It *can* be. As long as you're going to be *good.*"

My nipples were just painfully hard; my panties simply sodden.

"*That?*" I said, not entirely able to keep the tremble from my own voice, "Was *Level One.*"

He twitched a little in my arms and I tried again to sooth him.

"It goes to *Level Ten*," I whispered, as if telling him a terrible secret which I had only just learned, which was not really that far from the truth—although whether one said "terrible" or "wonderful" was a bit of a judgment call.

"You're going to help me," I implored him, "*aren't you?* You're not going to—" I held him tight in reassurance, but there was still a quick shudder through my thighs of . . . I'll call it *ambivalence*, "—you're not going to *make me* do that, are you? Huh? *Are you?*"

I felt him nodding hurriedly against my shoulder, in obvious panic; then I felt him shaking his head back and forth—clearly not sure what the "right answer," or the right physical gesture, was.

Well.

He was trying.

But . . .

I couldn't help but wonder.

Did I *want* him to succeed?

Really?

Because . . .

That fast and intense *convulsion* of pain?

From Level One?

The flood of pleasure it flowed through me was just . .

.

It was simply *Heaven.*

That I might be able to step him, inexorably-upward, from Level One to Level Ten?

I hugged him a little more; I kissed and reassured him; I told the nurse we would probably be ready to go home soon—if he could just retrieve the property bag for us?

And I'd be right back—I promised.

I'd get my husband up and dressed.

I'd fill his prescriptions.

I'd take him home.

Oh!

Of course!

I went into the bathroom, stuffed my mouth with a wad of rough and dry *institutional* paper towels: *just* enough to muffle *my* screams of ecstasy, as I frigged myself to three *painfully* deep orgasms, imagining the *unthinkable* pleasure of jolting my husband at Level Ten.

I could *all-but-feel* his body, helplessly flopping, like a landed fish, pained by and paying for his seemingly endless *Cock Crimes*.

I was *pretty* sure he would present me that opportunity.

On a silver platter.

Perhaps one of the reasons that I loved him as much as I did.

We have odd relationships.

Yes.

We do.

What more lovely thing could there be?

Beyond someone who pushes *your* buttons?

Well . . .

Then there's someone who gives you an excuse to . . . push *their* buttons.

To the point of pain—and then . . . *so* far beyond!

So . . . *Who's* Paranoid?

Clearly?

Either we didn't "coordinate this right," wife and me, or she was just immediately and committedly deaf, dumb, blind, and amnesiac.

We had—I *thought* we had; I thought we'd written into our wedding vows—a *deal.*

Lil' bit o' sumpin'-sumpin' *on the side?*

Everybody being discrete?

Not just that we didn't *ban* that?

I *thought* that was something we had explicitly *authorized.*

Thought that was pretty clear.

Point was, of course: *Discrete.*

Point was, above all else: Be *respectful* of the other person, how you make them feel, how you make them *look* publicly.

And . . . I'll grant: The argument that I had *not* been entirely discrete?

Pretty strong argument.

Disrespectful?

I—

I just—*clearly!*—don't know.

That was certainly not my *goal,* being disrespectful?

But . . . here I am: *Dick-Chipped.*

More-than-Obvious that . . . there'd been a little less "consensus" than I thought there was; just . . . not a great deal of *Peace in the Valley.*

No.

And that chip?

Never mind anything else?

Never mind projecting forward to . . . whatever my future might be?

It was . . . "reading" what it was "reading."

Read that I was hard?

Made sense.

Read that I was . . . *a-rubbin'*?

Made sense.

Read that I was . . . with someone else?

Well . . . my wife was there or she wasn't.

No arguing with that at all—she knew where she had and had not been.

But.

The *Shock* Button?

I know "a little bit" about my wife.

What's going on now?

This is—*Swear-to-God*, bet my life on it; I can see—just wetting her panties.

The level of control.

The feeling of power.

That . . . rattling of power through her body.

Not just that she "likes" that?

No.

It's a high.

What *she's* getting is *high.*

What *I'm* getting?

I deserve it or I don't: Different question.

What I'm getting?

Well . . .

Just . . . *jolted.*

But . . . what's going on now?

The deeper, sadder, more difficult reality?

Yeah.

I'm getting off on it, too.

Being jolted.

Yeah.

For now, anyway . . .

Because . . . she's been slowly ratcheting up; doesn't seem like the "dosage" ever goes down.

Among her other goals, I just *know*, she wants to get me to *Max Shock*.

She's been setting traps, assigning me semi-impossible things to do—or to avoid; nudging the standards and bending the rules.

And—the most fiendishly ingenious part of this?—whenever I even *hint* that she might not be playing fair . . . *that* constitutes "a problematic level of disrespect," a grave violation which—of course!—simply requires further . . . escalation.

Oh! You Want One Too?

What I've always just loved about Meryl—go back to high school, or even earlier—is that she's never had either the desire or the capacity to say anything other than what she absolutely believes, what she's thinking, what she's feeling, what she wants.

When we were growing up, most people took that as "a Rich Girl thing."

That's never what I thought it was.

Drove her own parents to distraction.

Start there.

If it was just that she was being manipulative—she was always, as my Gramma would put it: whip smart—she would have dialed it up and down with precise calculation and absolute efficiency.

Not what she did.

Nowhere even close.

It was never that she just "threw a switch."

Rather, Meryl was just always Meryl: 24/7/365.

That *scared* men—her father very much included.

Forty just around the corner?

The only word she's ever used is "boys," her rejection of the very possibility of "male maturation" an Iron Rule she'd put into place in 7th grade, and never felt merited changing.

But if she scared her father?

It was completely obvious, early on, that—beneath the thinnest possible scrim of obligatory parental judgment—her mother had always taken a great deal of vicarious pleasure from Meryl's "antics."

13

"So," Meryl was saying to me—the pitcher of Margaritas running low, her *Salade Niçoise* toyed with and damaged but largely uneaten, "how do you *re-charge* him?"

I was a little flustered ordering a second pitcher—and so fast.

But then, I'd had barely half a glass of the first pitcher.

"*That's* your question?" I asked when the waiter had retreated.

Meryl nodded calmly.

Someone who didn't know her might have thought she was being ironic; I knew that she was pretty much "launching a research project," intentions quite serious.

"Danny been . . . behaving badly?" I asked, checking on the status of the—most recent—fifteen-years-younger *Boy Toy* that Meryl had something very close to tied up in her basement.

She rotated her, mostly empty, glass on the cardboard trivet, slowly swirling the ice.

She daintily plucked a little flake of tuna from her salad, contemplating it briefly before popping it into her mouth and chewing pensively.

She watched our waiter return and swap out the pitchers, poured herself a full glass and sipped.

"Well . . ." she said slowly, "If—just suppose—I wanted to go from . . . renting to buying?" She looked at me, requiring a nod; I nodded gravely, "I would certainly want to understand the full menu of . . . control options, before doing so."

I poured myself a glass from the new pitcher, filling it to the top—whether I would or could finish it, I wanted to "preserve my options."

"Those are the circumstances under which you'd consider getting married?"

I knew as I said the words that I was being not merely "judgy" but full-on hypocritical.

Why were we even talking about this, after all?

What had *I* done?

Hadn't made it an engagement requirement?

Arguably an error on my part—the question of "available technology at the time" put aside.

Meryl didn't answer.

She left me to my own cascade of thoughts, while she plucked an olive from her salad, contemplated it as if it might be an alien species, finally popped it into her mouth, chewed languorously, eyes steady on mine.

"You there yet?" she finally asked, voice remarkably soft and neutral.

I nodded hurriedly, took my own long sip, just about swallowed the last chicken finger whole.

I explained various "maintenance procedures" in a slightly embarrassed murmur, then, rummaging through my purse for a pen, scribbled on a napkin and handed it to her.

"That's the website," I said.

Meryl nodded, closed her eyes, smiled, folded it and tucked the napkin into her bra.

Well that was—

The waiter—maybe fifteen years younger than us?—landed a tray on a tableside stand, set up by a busboy, began both distributing and retrieving plates, looking a little nervous, his eyes flickering metronomically in the direction of Meryl's cleavage.

Got it: Performance understood.

She watched him stride off, her face both serious and a little wistful.

"Figure he's probably gay?" she said. "Really not . . . interested or accessible; no real possibility there?"

I turned, watching over my shoulder as he ducked behind the bar, and then bumped open the swinging door to the kitchen with a skinny hip, and disappeared in a cloud of steam and noise. But—just before that?—glancing over *his* shoulder.

At Meryl.

"Looking to add to the stable?" I asked.

She shrugged, flicked a radish off her plate and onto the floor, drawing a disdainful glance from a nearby table.

"One always . . . *looks*," she said slowly. "But," snapping back into focus, "tell me about this website—and about how you're doing with the . . . *domestication*—finally!—of your husband."

Don't Ask . . . Don't Tell

Who am I supposed to talk to?

And what, *exactly*, am I supposed to say?

Who really knows me? Who do I really *want* to know me?

'Dullah's my closest friend—back to high school.

His parents got into the Nation of Islam thing, around the time he was in middle school.

They re-named him "Servant of God," *Abdullah.*

High school? Names get a little bent around.

Not to mention the fact that—messing with a sacred name?—he was the least religious person I'd ever met, in full-on rebellion against his parents, his name, just about everything else, too . . . but not quite sure where to take that.

Now?

More than a little "backsliding," way I saw it—with a little bit of a *Malcolm X* angle to it: him feeling more and more drawn to *True Islam*, rather than the, literal, flying saucer cult that is *The Nation.*

"So, we're meeting in a bar," I said, "but you're tellin' me you're done with alcohol? And that's it for pork, too?"

If he was blushing, figuring that out was more a matter of physical cues than anything else.

"Thinkin' about things . . ." he said with an easy smile. "And—you got a little weed maybe?—not lookin' to give up . . . *everything.* Not just yet—Koran's okay with weed, you know."

"What's her name?" I asked, not bothering not to sound skeptical, inquisitive, or judgmental.

"Oh, *Man!*"

"No, no!" I said. Tapped him on the chest for a moment; leaned in, banged him gently, forehead to forehead. "We bein' straight? We *not* bein' straight? Let's just . . ."

He cupped the back of my head for a quick minute, made a grunt of acknowledgement, mumbled *Fareesha* in my ear—pretty sure that's what he said, anyway.

I stood upright, drew back just a little, flagged the bartender.

"Friend here is just *desperately* thirsty for another club soda," I told her. "You can maybe help him out?"

"Why I came to work today!" she cried cheerfully. "Lemon or lime? She asked 'Dullah. "Pick your poison!"

"Lime's just fine," he murmured—always fun to see a man that big go shy.

She nodded, scooped in some ice, squirted in some club soda, pinched and dropped a crescent of lime, landed the glass before him with a napkin and a straw.

"We good?" she asked, something about her sudden focus and stillness just a little disconcerting.

'Dullah got still too, gave a little sigh.

"Yes ma'am, we are," he said evenly. "Yes ma'am we are."

And now . . .

I'm gonna tell him *what* exactly?

Little bullshit melanoma thing on my leg? Just lettin' ya know: that's gone.

Happy thing; absolutely; clean biopsy, too!

And *oh-by-the-way* . . .

My Dear Wifey—while I was, briefly, *outta-this-world?*—took the opportunity to install some *accessories* that I've been finding a little . . .

Buzzy and burdensome?

Life altering?

Shockingly . . . attention-getting, scary, and in some way . . . compelling?

"Bitch *Dick-Chipped* you?"

18

"How does everybody suddenly know this word?" I asked, my voice sounding pathetic even to me, wishing he might have been just a little bit more quiet, hoping that I was imagining the little head-jerk, I am absolutely positive, the bartender just did.

"So, Muslims do circumcision," 'Dullah began, staring at his club soda as though there was any possible way it was going to help. "And when *my* parents . . ."

Fuck!

I know, I know. I. *Know!*

Bad-fucking-thing, get chopped at twelve: up there on the Top Three List of "Worst Intros to Puberty *Ever.*"

"And she—us hittin' forty now about a week from Thursday?—she had you . . ?" He drank down half of his club soda. "*That's* just . . . *Damn,* Man! That is *cold!*"

"Kinda burns, really," I managed to mumble.

'Dullah flagged the bartender again.

"My Man here," he said, looking at her like he was delivering serious and precise medical information and instructions, "he wants *whatever-the-fuck* your top-shelf Bourbon is? Wants you to just pour it over his head, shampoo him with the shit?" 'Dullah put a hundred-dollar-bill on the bar, "we gonna just go ahead and do that, huh?"

She took the hundred.

She smiled.

Then she said, "Twenty-five a shot for the top shelf; twenty-five for me. He wants me to pour it on his head? I don't give a dusty fuck where it goes. But, just so we're clear? He wants conditioner? That's extra."

"And thank you for your service," 'Dullah muttered as she walked away. "And," turning back to me, "sorry for your pain, my Brother, *so* sorry—although . . ."

He stopped there.

For which I was grateful.

Very. Grateful.

Not feeling like what I most needed, at that particular moment, was to be told, to be reminded, how I'd fucked up.

I *know* I fucked up; I know *how*.
Story of my life.

What Have *You* Done?

I was allowing myself a little . . . *wiggle* room; that's true.

Not *quite* that I would pummel my pussy with a vibrator or a dildo as I shocked him?

That was a . . . not-infrequent *later-the-same-day* post-script?

Something for him more to sense—or, on rare occasion, to hear—not something he was given permission to witness.

Or: not yet, anyway.

There was still *some* standard—some form, some ritual—that required at least a *semblance* of attention, if nothing else: a degree of respect for the increasingly Pavlovian nature of what I was doing to him, however blunt, obvious, overt, or explicit it might be.

I'd *ring-his-bell*.

He didn't necessarily salivate at that trigger?

Well . . .

We have—women anyway—more than one mouth, more than one kind of appetite to be sated.

And—of course—more than one way to salivate.

He got shocked; I got wet.

Seemed like a more than fair trade to me.

We'd reached Level Five.

That midpoint, I had been told, was a crucial and delicate juncture.

"We assume neither that you do or do not fish," my web-counselor wrote, with gender-careful equanimity. "If this is obvious and repetitive for you, I apologize. The way we often put it: There is a point at which landing a fish, a

21

good-sized, energetic, fish, a potential *trophy* fish—one that you think may be, if you will excuse the metaphor, *mountable*—requires a little less brute force, or even technological sophistication, and a little more patience and . . . guile."

Guile.

Well . . .

I've never been—never aimed to be, never will be— Meryl.

However: Learning to be tactful, by watching the *Queen of Blunt?*

Perhaps less that I've "studied at her feet" and more that I have—for a good couple of decades now—not just surveyed but analyzed the human wreckage that she's left in her wake.

Tempted, now and then, to fish some broken pieces out of her *detritus* and . . . play with them?

Yes.

Never done it.

No.

Better to learn.

Better to wait.

Better to attract, buy, or—as perhaps I was now doing—*design* one's own toys.

That I had waited was feeling, day by day, more and more, like one of the best decisions I had ever made.

Level Five brought him—literally *dropped him*—to his knees, before me.

At which point, with him looking up at me in just *gorgeous* fear and confusion, I gave him—for the first time *ever!*—the *privilege* of watching me masturbate, my hands under my bathrobe, but over my panties, nothing of "lascivious appeal" visible to him, nothing but the gut-wrenching pleasure that his pain simply rattled through my body.

It wasn't that I *had* to go to my knees; I could have remained standing.

I was making *very* explicit choices.

"Bringing myself down to his level," looking into his eyes, the fingers of one hand knotted in his hair—as tightly and as *painfully* as possible—my other hand scrabbling with frantic urgency over the soaked crotch of the silky white panties I had permitted him to sniff but not to touch.

My web-counselor had focused on two primary points. So did I.

There is the primacy *of your pleasure,* she had written.

And there is your pleasure *in his pain.*

Show him both: Leave. No. Doubt.

About what you are feeling; about why *you are feeling it.*

About what he *is feeling; about* why *he is feeling it.*

About . . . what matters.

About: The only. *Thing. That matters.*

In the past; in the present; into the inevitable *and* endless *future.*

The only.

Thing.

That.

Matters.

YOUR.

PLEASURE.

Indeed.

No.

I had not.

He could've had no *possible* doubt.

Femdom Wife Takes Control, Book II:

Teaching Lessons & Learning Rules

Technical Support

"It's less that we're rebooting him—although we are—and more that we're installing a new operating system. Think of it that way."

Danarla was black and couldn't have been much over thirty, dressed in the *precision-casual* manner one would expect from a therapist: the therapist of my dreams; the therapist of my husband's nightmares; marriage counselor, life coach—tech support.

"You play with a new toy for a few weeks," she'd said, with an understated but understanding smile, "but then, at some point, you put it to work. You figure out—you make—the rules, you figure out *what-works-how*. Speaking of which," she added, "as we go along, you might find that there are a few plug-ins and accessory packs you might want to consider."

I saw myself frown briefly, in the little box at the upper righthand corner of my computer screen, where my own picture was reflected back at me.

"No, no, no!" she said hurriedly. "No additional cost! We promised that; we keep our promises. However you want to extend the system, whatever options we have: they're free."

My picture showed that I was relieved.

"So!" she said. "You have taken control of his penis away from him. I assume that you have been rigorous in having him exercise—*and improve!*—his oral abilities?"

I nodded.

"And they *have* improved," I agreed.

"Good! Have you permitted him intercourse?

27

Why would that be the embarrassing part for me?

I had.

Once—since I'd had him *Dick Chipped.*

I felt somehow guilty about it.

She gave a me a smile that was surprisingly sly.

"Think you did something I never heard about anyone doing before?"

I told her in a rush, afraid I'd stop myself if I didn't: I'd let him fuck me.

"Only once!"

With me in the dominant position—*of course!*—good cowgirl that I have become.

And I had triggered—and immensely increased the intensity of—my gut churning string of orgasms by giving him four, quick shocks, as I rode him, ramping up from level three to level seven in a fast sequence that had him bucking and bugged-eyed beneath me as I screamed in pleasure.

That amped up her smile.

"Been there, done *that,* Sister!" she said with enthusiasm.

"You?"

"Can't explain what you don't understand; can't understand what you don't live."

"Wow! I'm— *Wow.*"

"Okay, then," she said brightly, "you own his dick; now you're going to rename it."

"Like . . . *Sir Cums-Too-Fast?*"

"Hah!" she laughed. "We can fix that! Got an algorithm. But, no, I mean it's not 'a dick,' 'a cock,' 'a tool,' now; it's his *wee wee* or *pee pee* or *weenie* or *peenie.* It's not something he's proud of anymore; it's something he's embarrassed about."

"Psychological warfare." I saw myself smile appreciatively on the screen.

She nodded at this, but then amended what I'd said.

"Yeah—really?—it's retraining or reprogramming, something closer to that."

I must have looked a little unsure.

"The war? Sister, you won that when you got his poor little pee pee chipped.   Terms are always the same: unconditional surrender. We're in the *post*-war period now, now that you've locked up—or shocked up—his *post!* It's a brave new world. *Oh, yes!"*

There was something of a wicked edge to the glee reflected back at me from the top righthand corner of the computer screen.

I liked that.

A quick spurt of satisfaction and anticipation dampened my panties.

"Tell it, Sister!" I murmured. *"Tell it!"*

Assignments

It was clear that she was getting . . . guidance; it was clear that she was following some sort of program; it was clear that I was in even deeper trouble than I had initially imagined.

And I had imagined some pretty troubling stuff when I woke up from dermatological surgery and discovered that my wife had *Dick Chipped* me.

The first couple of weeks, post-surgery, had been a little rowdy and ragged.

I'd had affairs—I'd thought we had a *deal* about that—and she was angry, angrier than I had really understood. In the beginning, it had felt like she was a cold-eyed cat, using a captured mouse for hockey practice, batting me around, caroming me off walls, restraining herself from seriously damaging me—so the games could continue—but sometimes having trouble holding back.

And then—maybe two-and-a-half weeks in—things seemed to snap into focus.

She got serious, sat me down in the living room—literally "on the carpet," at her feet—and "read me the rules."

She'd taken off her pantyhose on returning from work; her skirt had ridden up a bit when she sat; I had a view of her gooseflesh-pebbled thighs, her pussy a blurry outline above—I'd swear I could smell, as well as see, her excitement.

She'd given me a brief cock shock.

"I'm up here," she'd said with soft menace, redirecting my attention.

I'd yelped and murmured an apology.

This was *Tough Love,* she said, a last-ditch attempt to save our marriage.

Did I want to remain married?

I did.

Just no hesitation at all; my heart sank at the thought of losing her.

I loved her; simple as that.

I now somewhat feared her, as well; somehow that didn't cancel out the love.

In some ways?

If I'm being honest with myself?

In some—likely sick—way?

Her ever-increasing control over me made me love her even more, tinged that affection and need with an odd measure of awe—and a little *frisson* of fear.

My pledge of love for her yielded a sweet and sour smile and a thoughtful hum.

Then she reached to the side table, picked up her tablet, and read me a list of requirements and obligations, delineating how my life would be.

I was to quit my job.

I was to be stripped of my assets and of independent access to money.

I was to spend most of my time at home—generally, for some odd reason, wearing a shirt but nothing else: bare-butt and shoeless—performing whatever tasks she assigned me.

"You will have sexual assignments, as well," she all but purred, slowing down and going a little uncharacteristically heavy-lidded.

She gave me another quick cock shock.

"*Ouch!* What was *that*—?"

With the tips of her fingers, she crawled the hem of her skirt up to her hips, exposing her pussy, beginning to redden and swell in its forest of curls.

I only dared look for a second.

"That was for no reason whatsoever," she said languidly. "That was because shocking your little *wee wee* gives me pleasure."

I was excited by the way she was talking to me, by what she was doing to me, by what she planned to do to me.

I don't—

I can't explain why.

My cock began to stiffen.

And was quickly auto-shocked down again, which made me moan in frustration.

She reached out and stroked my head tenderly.

"I know," she said, in the sympathetic voice one would use to comfort a child, "it hurts. Doesn't it?" she prompted me, softly at first, then with more of an edge. "*Doesn't? It?*"

"It does," I whispered.

"Good," she said with a gentle smile. "I'm glad."

I had started out feeling self-righteous, feeling wronged; but the more she punished and controlled me, the more genuinely penitent I felt, the more I *knew* that I both deserved and *needed* to be treated this way.

"I'm going to make you good," she had assured me in the first days after the surgery.

I had come to believe her.

I would have twenty-four hours to decide, she told me: stay or go.

If I "went" she would give me the name of a couple of surgeons who could remove the Dick Chip. And . . .

"If you stay," she said softly, gently pulling me forward and guiding my face to her pussy, "you will perform all of the services, domestic and sexual, that you are assigned, and you will still be punished on a regular basis."

I began to lap at her, as she had coached me: *oral service*, as she called it, no longer a haphazard matter of tongue-lashing and sucking.

Mashing my face tightly against her for a moment, with a palm at the back of my head, she gave me three quick cock shocks that made me yelp, the sound and vibration eliciting from her a sigh of the deepest satisfaction.

The sound was a music I was deeply proud of having wrung from her body.

Evangelizing

"Well you can't spay a dog you don't own," Meryl said. "*Although* . . ." her face took on a thoughtful expression, "if you find a *stray,* you can pretty much . . ."

She trailed off.

Well that was just *Vintage* Meryl, wasn't it!

There we were, in her pristine living room, one side of it a wall of glass that looked out over her huge, sloping backyard, a decanter of martinis on the coffee table before us, along with a platter of elegant Danish, open-faced, sandwiches—which had been prepared by her ruggedly handsome cook, and delivered to us by her buff young "houseboy," who, as Meryl put it, "is a simply outstanding multi-tasker. Aren't you, Dear?" she'd asked, the question clearly rhetorical, running her hand lightly up the back of his thigh, as he leaned to land the sandwiches.

He'd stood upright, colored a little, but not answered.

When he turned to go—dismissed with a squeeze and a pat on his ass—it was quite obvious that it was more than his posture that was . . . upright.

Meryl had a series of unbending *rules-for-staff.*

One was that they—male staff, at least; and her household staff was almost entirely male—were forbidden underwear. She'd had a party several years back—a Girl's Night In, she had called it—for which they were forbidden clothing of any kind, save strategically placed ribbons. And her "Blue Ribbon Gardener" at the time was . . . impressive.

"He tills the soil well and thoroughly!" she'd cried on more than one occasion.

I'd *Dick Chipped* my husband; unmarried, she would start a collection of *Dick Chipped* men, create a little kennel in her backyard, take them out when she wanted to use and abuse them, put them back when she was done; no muss, no fuss.

Perhaps she'd start with staff.

That would almost make sense.

Well . . . *Meryl-Sense,* anyway.

She leaned back on her white leather couch.

Meryl had a thing about mono-color rooms: The living room was white; the kitchen was a headache-inducing shade of highlighter yellow.

She had two bedrooms—one black and one red—and *commuted* between them, as she put it, depending on her mood.

Pity the poor unprepared boy who wound up in the black bedroom: dark things happened there, I knew. And pity the poor unprepared boy who wound up in the red bedroom: *partying bright* with Meryl could be almost as scary as *partying dark.*

"So, are you getting a commission?" she asked me with a laconic smile.

"Am I—*what?*"

"Well, Honey, you've sold *me.* This isn't just sex tech—*clearly!*—it's a full-on lifestyle. Hell: It's a damn religion!"

"I'm not— *You* don't even—"

I paused, blinked at what I had thought but not said.

What had come to mind was not that Meryl didn't "have" a man, nor that she wasn't married; what I had thought but not said was: But you don't even *own* a man!

My web counselor, Danarla, had said—and so far she'd never been wrong—that it wasn't just my husband that was being re-trained; it was me, too.

"You'll shed old habits," she'd said. "You'll write new scripts. You are *In Charge!* Gonna *own that,* Girl! Gonna come to love it. They all do."

"To Hell with getting a job as their Chief Marketing Officer—or whatever!" Meryl said, slowly rotating her highball glass, making the olives spin.

That had been nowhere on my agenda.

"We have the makings of lovely little cult here," she cried. "We need to go forth and *Spread the Good News!*"

Restrictions

"Your *armpits?*"

She didn't look smug; she looked something closer to serene than calm.

She'd been doing week-long "focus trainings," in which I was largely restricted to one zone of her body: her feet, her legs, her back; more massage with that latter part; mostly oral attention just about everywhere else; sessions that lasted more than an hour—often multiple times per day.

At the end of each seven-day cycle, I was permitted—I was required—to cum by rubbing against "the body area of the week," which, whether I was sawing between her thighs or frantically trying to achieve friction on the small of her back, made me feel like a desperately horny puppy.

I wasn't permitted to use my hands.

Then I was required to lick her clean.

She had become increasingly more . . . I'll call it *stingy* with the parts of her body that she permitted me to see: when, where, and for how long; sometimes when I was—as she called it—*servicing* her, she would require that I wear a blindfold.

Sometimes I would catch a furtive glimpse of leg or cleavage, a flash of her body as she exited the shower—as her towel or bathrobe billowed or swirled—a little slip of skirt or blouse, and she'd give me a quick jolt and a scolding.

"No *peeking!*" she'd say sternly, as though I were a little boy.

Of course, she knew, with exquisite precision, when I got hard: in what situations, triggered by what stimulus; degree and duration of inflation; the app kept records.

"Nasty little pee pee!" she'd fume, mashing the red button a few times, deflating me with a few fast "bee sting" shocks.

Peeking?

Pee Pee?

This confused and—confusingly—excited me.

And I *did* feel, in ways both subtle and obvious, as if I were being regressed.

Masturbation was—of course!—strictly forbidden, and, given the Dick Chip, for all practical purposes, impossible.

There was no longer anything faintly resembling "free access" to her body—*to my wife's body!*

The act of "petitioning or pleading" was particularly frowned upon.

Anything that she—for whatever reason or whim; for no reason at all—deemed to be "pawing" was a punishable offense.

That seemed to be growing: the list of punishable offenses.

And the intensity of the punishments was increasing as well.

"Yes," she said calmly, "for the next seven days, your primary focus of worship will be my armpits." She didn't even raise her eyebrows—in mock offer of receptivity to question or comment—she simply walked away.

I *had* noticed, over the previous week or two, that she had stopped shaving one armpit; asking why, or thinking about this too much, had simply seemed too dangerous.

She had taken to saying, about all manner of things: "When you are to know, you will be told."

And now, while she hadn't told me, I knew—as I was beginning to see all kinds of things spool out before me—at the end of the week: I was going to fuck one of her armpits.

And then, having been doing diligent tongue practice for the previous six days, I would lick her clean.

She stopped wearing deodorant, which, initially confused me.

This was a health matter, she informed me tartly: I was to be humiliated and degraded and sexually subservient— something that I had earned, she told me on a regular basis.

"You behaved irresponsibly with your pee pee; it is no longer yours to control!"

But she drew the line—one of the few she drew—at what she deemed excessive or imprudent chemical exposure.

I suspected as well that there was a pheromonal component to this act: to most of them, really. She was— literally!—rubbing my nose in, having me run my tongue over, every nook and cranny of her body.

The bouquet of scents was almost overwhelming.

She was never rank but she was often pungent: I sometimes had trouble distinguishing whether I was being made dizzy by panic or by the odd little, jagged, shards of pleasure that more and more of her abuse was sparking in me.

She washed her armpits, morning and night; she wasn't unclean.

But my most intense and extensive sessions of "pit worship" were on awakening—sometimes coming suddenly out of sleep to find that she was leaning over me in bed, trapping my face under her arm—or on her return from work.

In both cases: before she washed.

A day or two before the end of the cycle, I noticed that she had stopped shaving the "smooth" side as well.

And the dilemma she was setting up for me became clear: there would be no smooth skin on offer; "the hairy pit" would feel better than what was rapidly becoming "the stubbly pit," which had rapidly taken on the texture of sandpaper; but licking it clean, sucking my own cum from that little patch of curls, would be the more repellant task.

My guess was that this would be a rare instance in which she gave me a choice.

She did.

I chose stubble.

"Because licking the hair clean would be harder?" she asked.

I nodded hurriedly.

But she persisted.

"*And?*"

I think she knew before I said it.

"I'm beginning to enjoy the pain," I half-whispered.

She nodded in satisfaction, gave a little confirmatory hum, seeming not at all surprised.

Then she turned and walked away.

Intensifying

"We don't refer to it as Cock & Ball Torture," Danarla, my *Chip Coach,* said placidly. "CBT is more of a recreational infliction of pain; what we are doing here is part of the larger training program—or it is if you want it to be, anyway."

It had been the most incredible two months of my entire life.

Asking was no longer a meaningful part of my life; I simply instructed.

Choice was *my* prerogative; obedience was his iron rule.

Guilt or regret—as I pushed him ever-lower—were in my rearview mirror and fading fast.

It wasn't just that I felt powerful—I did; I was—it was how wonderfully calm and untroubled I felt, pretty much all the time.

Did aerobics.

Tried yoga.

Dabbled in meditation.

No comparison!

Those were—at least sometimes—temporary highs; my *life* now was on a higher plateau.

And whether it was my continuing to climb or him continuing to fall—to some degree it was obviously both—the exhilaration I felt, day to day, minute to minute, concrete act by concrete act, was just incomparable to anything I had ever experienced before.

I had the contents of the package that had just arrived spread out on the desk before me.

Danarla was walking me through the two new devices: what they did, how they worked, the best ways in which to deploy them.

"So this thin little rod," I was asking her, "goes—?"

"It's a urethral sound," she said. "Goes just where you'd think it goes."

"And the—?"

"Just look at it."

"—butt plug?"

"Goes—"

"Got it! And this is the control unit?"

"Right. You can use it manually or you can use it via the phone app, which gives you what we like to think of as 'remote control' capabilities."

"*Sweet!*" I said, feeling like a giddy kid on Christmas morning.

Oh, *thank you* Santa Claus!

I will be the *best* Bad Little Girl you ever saw in your life!

The other accessory I had ordered was a little more odd-looking: sort of a small sleeve or tube, peach colored, maybe an inch long, resembling what I imagine a severed foreskin would look like.

Near one end, the interior surface, perhaps a quarter inch in, had a ring of spines, like the fine, hair-like needles on a small cactus. The outside surface, more or less at the midpoint, had four, almost imperceptible, nipples.

The device was made of a rubbery material and, rolled between my fingers, I could feel the fluid inside.

"We send it to you already filled," Danarla told me. "The package should contain four syringes for refills; that should last at least six months."

"And you said the four drugs are—"

"Doesn't matter what they are. Think of them this way: there's *Up,* there's *Down,* there's *Numb,* and there's *Ouch!* That's all you need to know. Just snug it down over the head of his *pee pee*—it'll look kind of like his *little man* is wearing a scarf, top of the head kind of poking out, the tines should be

44

just under the corona—and the chip will recognize it and connect it to the app."

"And then—?"

"And then you're the *Puppet Mistress!* You want him hard, you want him soft? You want him numb, you want to give him a little extra sting? Once the device connects, those options will be added to your menu. Greatly increases your pleasure possibilities, your control options, and your range of training opportunities and modalities."

"Modalities!" I laughed.

"Got my script," Danarla laughed back at me easily. "Important to stay on it, define our terms, be clear."

"I'm all about clarity," I assured her.

"And control!"

"That too."

"Oh, Honey!" she said quietly, with a subtle shiver, "And *pleasure. So* much pleasure! It is just going to keep getting better," she assured me.

I felt a warm glow of satisfaction and anticipation; my pussy felt wet, swollen, and hungry.

"For me," I smiled, as much to myself as to her. *"For me."*

Femdom Wife Takes Control
Book III: Too Far?

But Wait—*There's More!*

It pretty much felt like she had *un*-circumcised me, rolling the rubbery, inch-long sleeve—or scarf or *faux* foreskin—over the head of my cock, leaving just the tip visible, covering the corona, and immediately . . . *pricking-my-prick*, with the rows of fine needles with which the diabolical thing was lined.

"There we *go!*" she said, smile tight and happy, eyes shining with excitement and satisfaction. "The next . . . *phase.*"

No point in asking what that meant—or what my new little *cock-scarf* would do—I would be told when I was told.

Didn't have to wait long at all: First I was *shown*.

She fiddled with her phone for a few long moments, trying to figure out a new menu, it seemed like—I had *really* come to fear that phone!

The fact that she showed a little flare of frustration—I knew from weeks-long experience—was not a good thing for me.

No.

Her frustrations—her upsets, her dissatisfactions, her irritations however petty, whatever the origin—they had found something between a "home" and a "solution."

Me.

If she was, in whatever fashion, unhappy?

49

I . . . felt her pain—or, more accurately?

She made me feel pain.

Calming for her; rather less so for me.

"Alright!" she said, finally, refocusing her attention. "Here's the new *music!*"

I didn't have time to puzzle over what she had said—but it became immediately and terrifyingly obvious that her "Cock Conducting" abilities and options had been expanded.

At base: There was *hard*, there was *soft*, there was *numbness* and there was *pain*—not completely new additions to "the orchestra" of control—and there were also "combination modes."

"This, for example," she cried happily, "is *hard* and *numb!*"

I blinked in surprise, looking down on the rampant cock I could no longer feel, as though a sensationless length of sawed-off broomstick had simply been grafted to my body.

"And then—" she said, and I yelped, "we can also add *pain!* Isn't that *wonderful?* Doesn't that open up just *limitless* possibilities?"

Well . . . obviously it meant she could fuck me—something she had mostly stopped doing.

She could make me hard enough to mount; she could *ride* to her heart's content; she could not just be sure that the only resultant pleasure would be hers, she could as well give me the little—or *big*—jolts of pain that seemed to *so* increase the intensity of *her* orgasms.

My mouth went dry and my throat went tight.

Neutrality would not be enough.

Clearly a response was being demanded; and there was not the slightest doubt regarding what that response simply had to be.

I ran my dry tongue over my dry lips, croaking more than whispering: "That's . . . *wonderful?*" Simply unable to completely commit to unalloyed enthusiasm.

There was a malicious quality to her smile of approval that made my heart skip a beat.

It terrified me.

And . . . it turned me on (and . . . it terrified me that it turned me on).

I saw my cock bob briefly, as if this had triggered a throb of blood. But—of course—I could feel nothing.

Was a Sunny Day

I hadn't, in the beginning, allowed myself to "trust it," to open myself up to the possibility that what I was embarking upon could be truly transformative.

I mean—pick up any women's magazine!—"Here's how to fix your husband" isn't anything particularly new or different. And—I mostly have to think—we keep getting *new* plans and programs and products and advice because . . . we can't seem to get it right.

Plenty of "War Games."

No shortage of "Plans of Attack."

Not a lot of . . . "Victory on the Ground."

And around we go again.

But *this* time!

Oh-my-fucking-God!

To hell with *Cosmo!*

Dick-Chipping?

This.

Works!

Just—*so*—incredibly well: the hardware, the software, the app, the counseling—the full shot, the whole package.

Plus—what *wouldn't* I have paid? but—it's "surprisingly affordable!"

And now I've become a late-night cable commercial, shilling for *fat-burners* and *cubic zirconium rings and bracelets.*

Hell with it!

I don't care.

Danarla is "happy with my progress."

Meryl is—a little scarily at this point—*enthused,* keeps talking about starting a cult.

Not the focus.

I was just living-the-dream: a husband under "proper control," pleasure on demand, done with explaining or arguing or hassling about . . . much of anything, really.

What else could a girl ask for?

"How broken do you want him?" Danarla asked.

"Broken?"

My own face, in the upper righthand corner of the screen, looked puzzled.

"Call it what it is. How much free will do you think he has left at this point? And how much do you want to permit him?"

"Permit him?"

I was echoing: yes.

"You wanna work it? You gotta own it," Danarla said, voice close to—but not completely—neutral.

"*Okaaaay,*" I said slowly—not really stalling—genuinely interested. "So . . . You tell me: What are my options?"

Danarla smiled.

In the upper righthand corner of the screen? I saw my own face.

And I saw it alternate between curiosity and something that looked a great deal like . . . worry.

Why should *I* be worrying about this?

I'd been working through a menu of choices for some months now; things had been going—spectacularly!—well.

Where was the problem?

I wasn't sure.

I just . . .

I found my own face a little confusing and disturbing.

"It's okay, Girl," Danarla said, voice a little brittle but going sympathetic. "Nothing you have to decide right now. But, little bit of time? You *are* gonna have to make some choices."

I watched myself nod at this.

Choices.
Yes.

You're Letting Her *What* Now?

I knew he'd find it, at least somewhat . . . *funny*, me being "*un*-circumcised," in part because—when his parents had joined the Flying Saucer Cult that is The Nation of Islam (the way he described it)—*he'd* been circumcised . . . *late*.

Like . . . as an adolescent.

"Which ain't," he always said, "when you want your dick chopped: when you can just—*Oh, so-too-much!*—be *there* for it. Do that shit when you're born, hopefully, you don't remember. Me? Oh, *Hell yeah!* I . . . *remember*."

"Feel it in your *bones?*" I always had to ask.

And he'd usually cuff me in the side of the head, us doing an obligatory comedy routine.

"Felt it in my *bone*, yeah! We *laughin'* about that now?"

"We are *not*," I always said; my line, on cue—as we both smiled just a *little* bit. "Of *course*: we are *not*."

'Dullah'd come to talk about that like it was a bitter joke because . . . any other way he talked about it just got too ugly, too angry, too fast.

"Every which way, Man," he'd say, "gotta make peace with your dick—you want it to make peace with you, anyway."

Sage advice indeed.

"And if I'd made peace a good little while back—" I said ruefully, my eyes grazing the stacked tiers of bottles behind the bar.

"—Maybe-might not be wearing that little *Dick-Scarf* you say she just put on you," he finished for me.

I wanted to change the subject.

57

"What's her name again?" I asked mildly—no way he wouldn't know who I meant.

'Dullah was drinking club soda—wouldn't split the pulled pork sliders with me; maybe that meant he was still with *whoever-she-was*, trying to be a good—more conventional, a *true*—Muslim, *The Nation* being something he'd split from as soon as he split from his parents.

"Fareesha," he mumbled—I think; never quite sure if I was getting her name right.

"And . . ?"

"And?" he said. "And, and, *and?*"

"'Fuck you duckin'?" I asked, knowing he didn't really want me to leave him alone. "You guys together? Not together? You blew it? You're gettin' married. I haven't told *you* intimate shit—like eleven seconds ago? *Spill*, Man! Who *else* you gonna tell?"

"Oh, my Brother," he said, a little slow and sad. "It's . . . it's *fuckin' complicated,* y'know?"

I put an arm—half-way—across his broad shoulders.

"I do," I said, in slightly sad solidarity. "I do. Spill it anyway. I'll catch up," *pretty* sure that I was telling the truth.

'Dullah looked at his club soda as though it had let him down; looked at the tier of alcohol behind the bar; he sighed.

"Yeah, okay," he said, sounding tired. "So, she has this *sister* . . ?"

I gave the bartender a quick little hand ballet, ordered another Bourbon.

Pretty clear this was going to take some time.

And—given what I had going on at home?—that was more than fine with me. I was *primed* to hear someone else's problems: nothing but *music* to my ears.

The Ride of Her Life

"What *time?*"

"It's not a complicated question," she said, eyes flashing with anger. "What time did you say you would be home?"

"Well . . . after work, but—"

"And you're out by five?"

"Well, yes, but—"

"And you were supposed to have dinner ready for me by 6:30?"

"Yes, and I—"

"And what time is it now?"

At least one question that had a clear and unequivocal answer—but not one that was going to help me in any way, shape, or form.

"I—"

She pointed to the living room clock on the wall.

"What time. Is it. *Now?*"

It was a little after 7:30.

Time had . . . gotten away from me.

I'd been drinking; 'Dullah'd had a story to tell.

He'd listened to me; I'd wanted to listen to him.

And so, yes, I was . . . late. *Dinner* was . . . late. I had . . . kept her waiting.

"Did you or did you not," she said, "make a commitment to me, regarding dinner?"

I hadn't thought of it as a promise or a vow; I'd thought of it as . . . a mealtime estimate.

Clearly . . . I'd thought wrong.

Hard not to feel that—her surface anger and upset notwithstanding—she was actually enjoying this in a variety of ways, that it wasn't giving her . . . a welcome excuse.

She pursed her lips and nodded.

Then she reached for her cell phone.

"I— *Wait!* Please don't—"

She'd turned and was striding away when she "hit the button" and just brought me to the floor, writhing; I don't know what sounds I made. No possibility whatsoever that there was the slightest shred of dignity to them.

At the doorway to the kitchen, she'd stopped and turned around, walked back a few steps, to stand over me.

She hit the button again and I simply keened.

"Clothes," she said curtly. "All of them. Off. Now."

Twitching and fumbling, I complied, unable to rise, dimly aware of her looming above me; I scrambled to get everything off, blindly throwing clothing to the edges of the kitchen, as though it hurt to have them in contact with my body.

Through a haze of pain, I saw her kick off her shoes, skin down her pantyhose and tear off her own panties, casting them aside as I had thrown off my own clothing.

Poking and prodding me with her bare feet, with her beautifully pedicured toes, she positioned me on my back, then loomed above, feet astride my chest, her anger incandescent and simply magnificent, phone still in hand, her face a rictus of angry pleasure.

Raising the hem of her skirt to her waist, exposing her hairy, swollen, and demanding pussy, her gleaming, wet thighs, she squatted—still, six or eight inches above my chest.

Her inner lips—darker and turgid, her angry clit at the apex—protruded through the puffy, swollen, pink, outer lips, entrancing me.

"*That*," she hissed, reaching behind herself to swat at my cock, "was Level Nine! You. Will. *Not*. Be. Disrespectful.

In this. Manner. *Ever.* Again," she said, swatting in rhythm, not always hitting with precision.

Then her attention went back to the phone she had kept firm in her other hand.

I felt myself . . . erect.

She shuffled down my body and lowered herself enough to just catch the head of my cock between those swollen hairy hungry lips, spearing herself with precision to a depth just millimeters below my dick-scarf.

Then I went numb.

And she began to perform a violent and spastic ballet that I could only observe with envy and awe—simply tortured by the fact that she had just switched off my ability to enjoy anything beyond the abstract idea of what was happening as she rode me.

She gave me a constant stream of low-level pain spikes; I gave the yelps and yips she seemed to want in response.

When she was clearly *close,* she leaned in lower, having popped open her blouse and torn off her bra, grabbing my hair and pressing my face to her breasts—which I needed no encouragement at all to suckle and, gingerly, to bite—grinding her clit on me violently, her breathing a raspy storm.

Phone still in her hand, she gave me three fast jolts of pain that made me thrust upward in a way that made her gasp in pleasure.

"*Six,* you bastard!" she hissed. "That was only *Level Six!*"

I had no answer; I had no words; I had . . . no idea what to say or what to do or how to feel or what to think: I was just the mechanical bull she was riding.

She had started wheezing as she ground on me; she brought her chest fully down on mine, brought her lips to my ear, bit my ear lobe until—I was sure—it bled.

"*I'm saving ten, I'm saving ten, I'm-saving-ten!*" she chanted—into my very brain it seemed—as she hit me with a fast succession of shocks that must have been "only" nine, roaring her orgasms until, amidst the *storm* of her seemingly-*endless* pleasure . . .

I must have simply blacked out.

No Such Thing as Too Far

Meryl, for all kinds of things—I *know* this; I've known it since childhood—is just the wrong person to ask.

Yes.

Ask her if grinding a man into fertilizer and using him to increase the size of your tomato plants is a bad thing?

Her most likely response would have more to do with the quality of the sauce you were trying to make from the tomatoes than the moral question of . . . men as fertilizer.

And, if you tried to—gently of course—prod her in the direction of an ethical and humane answer . . . you would likely just confuse or upset her.

"You're hurting him and it brings you pleasure," she said, re-stating—quite accurately. "And the question is . . ?"

I wasn't sure what the question was.

It wasn't exactly that I wanted to be challenged.

He'd done wrong—just pathologically and repeatedly!—and I was, just obviously, doing right. Pretty clearly: He had simply courted the consequences.

And now he had them!

He had been . . . was "brought to heel" the right term?

Tethered?

Captured?

Tamed?

I'm not sure that vocabulary matters.

He kept fucking up—but seemed to want to stay married. And I wanted to stay married to him, as well! Although, why exactly was getting a little fuzzy for me.

And I had—we had—found . . . a solution.

Wasn't that what we had to call it?

Yes, clearly—Dick-Chipped as he was—it wasn't entirely fair to say that he was making fully voluntary choices.

But . . .

The "ultimate opt-out" was always available to him.

He could just bail on the relationship.

He hadn't.

So: I was controlling him?

Yes.

Literally.

But: wanted, needed, got off on?

Something.

He stayed.

He accepted.

He . . . obeyed.

Which—tell the truth: in addition to the exhilaration of punishing and hurting him—was just deeply gratifying; seemed to me: for both of us.

"What are you . . . *fretting* about?" Meryl asked, her attempt to humor me both somewhat touching and gratingly obvious.

"What if I kill him?"

Just popped into my head!

Not sure how that could possibly . . .

Just popped into my head.

Meryl slowly lifted the cocktail shaker from the coffee table in front of the couch, refilled her highball glass, topped mine off, took a sip and shook her head—likely, I knew, because melting ice had watered down the martinis.

She looked at me coolly for a moment, sipped again.

"Well," she said, landing her glass and giving me her full attention. "Honey, three questions," she began, then reconsidered. "No," she said, picking up her glass again and taking a long sip, "four: Why? How? Could you get away with it? And," she lifted her glass again, drained it, "would that bring you pleasure?"

I like to think of myself as unflappable.

And I've known Meryl for most of my life at this point.

The reason that last issue was particularly horrifying?

It wasn't a matter of morality—not in private conversation anyway.

The problem was . . . I somewhat thought it might.

Or, at any rate, I couldn't find it in myself to immediately answer in the negative.

Meryl didn't seem to find that terribly troubling.

I did.

BONUS Chapter!
An Excerpt from Jon Zelig's duology:

Terms & Turns: Sex & Submission
Book I: Becoming a Good Boy

Chapter Five: Changes

There was a lot of adjusting, between Saturday and Tuesday when we both had to go back to work, and then into the week itself. More for me—as I felt the foundation of my life fall away beneath me.

I was in a perpetual state of uncertainty and anxiety, about what to do and how to do it, about whether or not I was "getting things right," although it came home to me quickly and repeatedly that there was an odd underlying dynamic that had some useful piece to it: I'd spent most of my adult life worrying about *getting things right*; at least now there was a clear, consistent—loving—controlling authority.

Once I knew how something worked, some piece of our new life, I could relax into it, at least a little.

The more paralyzed I was by *what am I supposed to do?* or angry about *it's not fair*, the worse things were.

The more I gave in to *this is just how it works*, the better I felt.

Being a little boy meant that there was no—grownup, real world—way to fight against a raft of problems, or things that I would normally get upset about, so I had to make peace with them as best I could.

She was generally quite self-assured: about what would be done, how it would be done, how things were going to be.

We had never argued a great deal or with problematic intensity.

But what I became aware of—as soon as it stopped—was that a great deal of our emotional energy had gone into a kind of low-level scorekeeping, minor tussling over authority, and the accompanying irritations when either of us *didn't get their way.*

She had always been a self-assured person, clear about what she wanted, open to reasonable discussion. I was surprised by how smoothly and unselfconsciously she switched into simply being in charge.

She told me what to do and I did it: No long, drawn out, carefully modulated discussion; no backwash of compromise or irritation; all kinds of things just took much less time and much less energy.

Of course, I *was* irritated—or confused or outright *frightened*—by some of the things she seemed to simply take for granted would happen.

And while I almost never said anything in complaint—was I helping her keep me churning in a maelstrom of emotion that, in some perverse way, I found reassuring? a balance to the new peace born of acquiescence?—she would often see my upset and preëmpt me, always in the same way: Stroking my cheek, sometimes kissing me softly, talking to me in a tone closer to what one would use with an upset toddler.

"*No,*" she would say sweetly and sympathetically, shaking her head, "it *isn't* fair, *is it?*" Then a sigh, as if in resignation at the injustice of the world—with which we would *both* simply have to grapple—and she would usually just walk away.

Or she would make an exaggerated pouty face, as if in imitation of me, then pet my groin affectionately—which I could barely feel through the chastity device whether I was clothed or naked.

"You be my good boy now," she would say, in mock seriousness.

It quickly came to feel Pavlovian.

Work was strange on Tuesday.

How could it possibly *have been otherwise?*

I was a little tentative and jumpy. I wasn't used to the chastity device yet, and my constant awareness of it, of how it rubbed against my clothing—*was it visible? could other people see it? weren't there changes in me that were glaringly obvious, as well? no one really seemed to notice*—the cycle I went through as the day went on, briefly forgetting and then being startled back to awareness when I thought of something erotic—almost any part of that long, confusing, and exciting weekend—and progress toward an erection quickly came up against the restraint.

It was physically painful, but there was also a frustrating ping ponging back and forth: between physical discomfort and the erotic charge of the constant reminder of what I had acceded to; between anxiety—that there was something just *deeply,* irredeemably, wrong with me, that people would immediately know and respond to this—and an odd germ of peace and acceptance; between frustration at the length of the day and some relief that I had a little time away from home to think.

The biggest mistake I made was to reflexively accept an offer from a colleague to "catch a quick beer after work."

Just a little more time and space before I go home; get my bearings, I thought.

But there were *so* many ways in which I hadn't really thought that through. . .

First off, Jimmy wasn't really a friend. He was just a guy from work. We had a beer before heading home—just the two of us or sometimes a couple of other people as well— every few weeks, but we didn't *know* each other in any real sense.

I had been somewhat distracted at work. No one had really seemed to notice—nobody said anything, anyway.

Now, foolishly, I'd put myself one-on-one with someone, the primary focus of their attention—the only distractions the background scenery of women, and sports on the TV over the bar.

That I was ill at ease, oddly jumpy, was immediately obvious, and something that I had no credible way to explain.

Just trying to *think* of something to say—just a little minor lie to brush the question aside—escalated quickly in my head toward crisis.

What could I tell him?

I was upset because of something at home?

Sick pet or relative?

Money worries?

Problems with my wife?

That last one, in particular, almost made me choke on my beer.

What an incredibly dangerous—and *stupid*—conversational door that last one would have been to open.

And, somewhere in the recesses of my brain, I had a niggling anxiety that she would somehow *know* that I had been "over-sharing" or engaging in—never really thought about it this way—disrespectful chatter.

I didn't want to *get-in-trouble.*

Best I could muster was a *cares of the world* sigh and a shrug.

"Ah, you know. . . . *stuff.*"

"*Tell-me-about-it,*" Jimmy muttered reflexively, an obligatory gesture of sympathy, flagging down the waitress to get us another beer.

The second problem was peeing.

The chastity device had a little slit at the tip, but it was almost impossible to pee *straight.* Maneuvering to line up with the slit was difficult; with my cock all scrunched up, there was no way to aim.

I had quickly learned that I would have to pee sitting down, having sprayed the toilet and the floor the first time I had tried it standing up with the device on.

She had stood there in the doorway to the bathroom, shaking her head in gentle disapproval.

"You get a mop and some cleaning spray," she'd said firmly. "Clean up your mess. Then we'll have to get you changed and—" she couldn't seem to stop a grin from breaking through, "—Mommy will have to teach you how to go potty again."

Sitting down.

And prepared.

Because the process was imperfect at best and required cleaning up. At home I had learned that I could wash myself in the shower or the sink, with the device on, and dry myself—*oh so carefully*—with the hair dryer.

I had felt a burst of gratitude when she prepped me for work, by saying that I would have to remember to always bring paper towels with me into the stall.

How did she know that?

"And you want to make sure no one sees you pee, don't you? That's *private*," she'd added, petting my groin. "You be my good boy."

If Jimmy hadn't noticed that anything of consequence was bothering me, he was just as unfazed by my shooting up from my chair and rummaging frantically for my wallet.

Can't pee?

Can't stay.

"Curfew?" he smiled at me.

A little shard of panic shot through me but then faded: almost everyone at work used that shorthand for getting home to their spouse.

Didn't mean anything.

To him, anyway.

I just nodded sheepishly.

"Yeah. Jeez. . . forgot. . ."

Jimmy just gave me a little four-fingered kiddie-wave goodbye and turned his attention back to his beer, the TV, and the waitresses.

Which brings me to the last—and *worst*—thing I did wrong.

I was late.

When I hustled up the front walk, she was standing in the doorway, looking through the storm door. She had her fluffy, white, terrycloth bathrobe on and, as I got closer and she opened the door to usher me in, I could see that she held a belt at her side, looped.

"Get in here, young man!" she said curtly, closing both doors.

"Do you have *any* idea how worried I've been?" she demanded, looking me full in the face. "You *know* that you are not allowed to be out alone after dark."

Did I "know" that?

"And you are *never* allowed to just change your plans, *willy-nilly,* without asking Mommy's permission. Do you understand me?"

"Yes. . . yes, Mistress Mommy."

I couldn't keep my eyes from flitting constantly to the belt she was holding.

"*I'm up here!*" she snapped redirecting me, making me look into her eyes.

"This is *not* acceptable," she said, rapidly unsnapping and unzipping my pants, shucking them, along with my underwear, down to my knees.

Pointing to the living room, she directed me to one of the corners.

"You go stand there for a while; think about what you've done."

I found a wave of relief, as I shuffled awkwardly to comply, in the fact that the living room curtains were drawn.

But the belt really terrified me.

After that fast initiating experience—when she had awakened me in the middle of the night dressed as if for work, formal and formidable—she had taken to wearing that specific bathrobe around the house. On rare occasions, she would be nude underneath; more often, she wore those large, white, full-cut cotton panties that reached almost to her navel.

No more sexy lingerie around the house.

But, of course, there was something furiously, and disturbingly, exciting about that.

And—how could this *possibly* be?—was there something about the cut of the robe or the way in which she wore it that made it momentarily gape or sway open, when she was walking, when she was sitting, when she was standing, when she was lying in bed?

I was in a near-constant state of erotic jitter, trying to see a flash of her cleavage, her breasts, her legs, her ass, those huge, plain, white, cotton panties.

On Sunday, she had leaned over to get something from a shelf on the refrigerator door; I had seen one of her nipples.

I had a fast rush of excitement at that.

Then she looked up at me quickly, gathering the robe tightly around her neck and said, as if in shock and outrage, "are you *peeking* at Mommy? Are you trying to look under Mommy's robe?"

"I—" in a hot flush of shame, I knew that I had to confess—and did so as rapidly as possible.

She nodded, pursed her lips, made as if to say something then seemed to reconsider.

"I appreciate that you told me the truth," she said softly. "But only *very-bad-little-boys* peek at girls, *especially* their Mommies. If you are supposed to see something, Mommy will show you. If you're not, then you need to not be naughty like that."

"Yes, Mistress Mommy," I murmured.

After the rush of excitement, a flash of shame, I felt a warm wave of relief at the fact that it didn't seem like she was going to punish me.

Chemicals, I thought in wonder; it was as if I were an orchestra and she the conductor.

And her clothing had been deftly re-arranged, both reinforcing her authority and making her alluring to me in a series of ways that tangled and confused me.

I didn't really want to think it all through; it was too daunting.

She had been *business sexy* that first night, a little glossy, brisk, and stern. You would notice her at the office—smoky stockings, high heels, skirt a little tight, blouse a little filmy—but she didn't look trashy or fetishistic.

But, from then on, at home, she had become—on the surface at least—almost the *antithesis* of sexy, a study in white cotton concealment: those big panties; that voluminous bathrobe; long, plain, white, sheath nightgowns that fell below her knees, no meaningful cleavage visible at the top.

Which was all *agonizingly* exciting, my heart skipping a beat when she reached up for something and I saw a fast flash of the crescent of soft skin at the edge of her armpit.

Why?

And then the fact that I was being turned on by—that I was beginning to *obsess* over—these little innocuous flashes of skin: *it was embarrassing.*

I was furtively trying to see—to *peek*—under these irreproachably chaste garments; I was ashamed by this—and confused.

Except, of course, *I knew.*

I knew *exactly* what it was.

And *she* knew.

And she fed and nurtured my feelings.

Could it have been only once?

Because, almost always, it was gentle chastisement—it could certainly not have been more than twice.

Instead of being stern or softly chiding me, she gave me what looked like a sly, shy, quick smile, leaned in, her hair just grazing my cheek, spoke softly and hotly into my ear, her voice a teasing sing-song, as if we were sharing a naughty secret, something that pleased and flattered her, though she knew it was wrong, and whispered urgently:

"You were peeking at *Mommy! Weren't* you?"

Then a quick nuzzling of my cheek, her nose wiggling playfully in my ear. "I know it's so, *so* hard," she breathed. "But you *try* to be a good boy."

I must have been standing in the corner for fifteen minutes, fretting about the belt, ominous on the couch, wondering if this was the time to put a stop to the whole thing, before she came back.

Stop.

Or Go.

No middle ground.

She came back in and sat on the couch. I heard the soft jingle of the belt buckle.

"Turn around," she said. "Come stand in front of me."

The robe was loose on top. Standing, it was hard not to look down at her breasts. At the bottom, the robe was parted so that one of her legs was almost fully exposed. I thought I might have seen a flash of her panties, but struggled not to look, to notice, to think.

"Are you trying to peek at Mommy again, young man?" she said sternly.

"No, Mistress Mommy," I said quickly.

"Do you know why Mommy is so angry?" she asked.

I felt like my nose was beginning to run.

Was I tearing up? I *really* had to pee badly.

"Because I was out late and didn't tell you—didn't ask permission?" I said in a rush.

The belt lay on the couch next to her and I fought not to look at it, just as I was trying desperately not to look at her breasts, her legs, her panties.

"That's right," she said. "Mommy was *very* worried. It was dark out and I didn't know where my little boy was. I was getting scared I might have to call the police."

"I'm sorry Mistress Mommy," I managed, trying to keep my voice from breaking. "I really, *really,* have to pee!"

"Mommy knows how beer works," she said with a tight smile.

Finally, I couldn't help looking directly at the belt and sobbing out the question, "Are you going to hit me with the belt?"

She paused—the length of three of my shuddering breaths—looking directly at me with an expression that I couldn't quite read.

She didn't seem to be thinking.

"No," she said finally, her expression softening. "Kneel down for Mommy."

It was awkward with my pants as they were; it was painful with my bladder so full.

She reached out and stroked the side of my face, my hair, my forehead.

"You know that Mommy loves you very much," she said quietly. "Mommy will *always* love you. Even though sometimes you make her angry or make her scared." She reached over to the belt at her side, placed her hand over the buckle. "Mommy doesn't ever *want* to use the belt," she said, pausing, making sure the threat was perfectly clear.

"But you have to be a *good* little boy. You have to be obedient, you have to be polite, you have to not do the nasty things that *bad* boys do."

She hesitated.

"I *know*," she said slowly, "you *think* all kinds of bad things. *All* kinds of bad. *Nasty*. Strange. Disgusting. *Embarrassing*. Scary. *Sick things*. Don't you?"

I was crying; I nodded abjectly.

"You don't have to be ashamed about that," she whispered, still stroking my face. "You have to *be* a *good* boy—and you have to listen to Mommy—but you can *think* anything you want."

"*Anything*," she said, after another pause and with some force. "It's okay. Mommy really needs you to understand that."

"I love you, too. . . I'm sorry I was bad, Mistress Mommy," I sobbed. "I didn't mean to make you worry. I won't do it again."

"There we go," she crooned. "*That* wasn't so hard, was it? Now we can kiss and make up."

I brought my face to hers, but she turned her head a little.

"Not on Mommy's lips," she said.

I stayed in contact with her cheek for a few moments, not wanting to move.

"Now," she leaned back slightly, parting the top of her robe just a little, but holding it against her skin. I could see more of her cleavage and her breasts, but not the nipples. "You may kiss Mommy here."

It was even harder for me not to linger there, but I felt like I was on the verge of actually wetting myself.

"Now," she said, her voice getting huskier. She parted the bottom of her robe, fully exposing both of her legs, the entirety of the white panties. "You may kiss Mommy on that *big* wet spot," she whispered.

"Just a quick kiss, no tongue, no lingering. Oh *gooooood boy*," she said.

As I obeyed, she first pressed my face tightly up against that damp and fragrant patch of cloth, rubbing the evidence of her arousal on my nose and my cheeks, then pushed me gently back, with what seemed like some regret.

"Go on now," she said, a little breathlessly. "You scoot to the potty. We don't want any accidents," calling after me as I quickly complied, almost tripping on my pants, "you wash your hands nice and clean, and brush your teeth, but you do *not* have Mommy's permission to wash your face."

The relief of peeing was just incredible. It wasn't an orgasm but it was damn close.

From down the hall, in our bedroom, came a ferocious pulse of wailing and then the intense keening sound of *her* orgasm, which seemed to go on forever, almost drowning out the steady buzz of her vibrator.

Excerpted from Jon Zelig's:

Terms & Turns: Sex & Submission
Book I: Becoming a Good Boy

Also Available in Audio Format

Thanks for Reading!

If you liked this: Write a Review!

If you didn't, please let me know why:

jonzelig@protonmail.com

The Zelig Family

Weird genetics? Something in the water? Odd family dynamics? Whatever it is . . . The Zeligs *do* seem to be a little . . . erotically obsessed. But each one in their own particular way:

Bram Zelig skews toward Paranormal Romance & Erotica.

Jon Zelig does Femdom, often w/ elements of age play, cuckolding & male chastity.

Joy Zelig—Jon's twin and mirror image—does more Maledom.

Zoë Zelig is softer; BDSM, Maledom oriented, but more romantic, something of a *Fifty Shades of Grey*-inflected focus on wealth & power.

Their characters tend to love one another and they have an ongoing interest in the moral underpinnings of power exchange: What's consent, where are the lines, who gets to judge—sexually or emotionally? What's public and what's private? When do pain and pleasure shade into damage?

They're trying to do what we all try to do: just . . . make it work.

www.amazon.com/author/bramzelig
www.amazon.com/author/jonzelig
www.amazon.com/author/joyzelig
www.amazon.com/author/zoezelig

Meet Jon Zelig!

Credit: Shutterstock

www.amazon.com/author/jonzelig

Jon Zelig writes about sexually intense, romantic, power exchange relationships: mostly Femdom; often in conjunction with T&D, D&S, FLR, Chastity Play, and Cuckolding.

Age Play is also a recurring theme: usually a *Wife-as-Dommy-Mommy*, disciplining and taking care of a *Bad-Little-Boy-Husband*.

Most of his work takes place in a contemporary setting: sometimes this is with an "alternative reality" skew; some is set in the near-term "Gynarchic Future."

No "adult babies," no diapers, no cribs; no incest, no violence, minimal compulsion; more psychological domination than physical.

A bit of hand, hairbrush, or belt: No whips or crops or canes.

Pinked—or reddened—bottoms, backs, and thighs?
Yes.
Bleeding, bruising, *damage?*
Dear, God(dess)!
No.
Almost always—the intensity of the roles they are playing notwithstanding?—his characters love and try to take care of each other.
Otherwise . . ?
What's the *point,* really?

jonzelig@protonmail.com

Meet *Joy* Zelig!

Credit: Shutterstock

www.amazon.com/author/joyzelig

Joy Zelig—Jon's *five-minutes-younger* twin sister—tends more in the direction of Maledom, as in ***Yes, No, Maybe: A Trilogy of Age Play Novellas*** or ***The Good Master,*** dabbling as well in lesbian romances like **Sexual Manners at the Manor**, which explores bisexual BDSM themes.

joyzelig@protonmail.com

Meet Bram Zelig!

Credit: Shutterstock

www.amazon.com/author/bramzelig

Bram Zelig—a cousin of the, erotica-writing, twins **Jon Zelig** & **Joy Zelig**, the former more Femdom-Focused, the latter more Maledom-Oriented—writes about the supernatural in a contemporary setting, erotica and romance threading through the tapestry of his work.

Vampires walk among us, thirsty for blood! And . . . sometimes hungry for love, sex, and a little compassion. Just because you have "biting issues" doesn't mean you're fundamentally bad! Just because you're supernaturally attractive, charming, and magnetic doesn't make you *good*— or necessarily the best person to get into a relationship with!

And . . . just because Love, Sex, Death (and *The Undead*) are serious topics? Doesn't mean there's never anything to laugh about. *Otherwise. . . ?* What's the *point,* really?

bramzelig@protonmail.com

Meet Zoë Zelig!

Credit: Shutterstock

www.amazon.com/author/zoezelig

Zoë Zelig read all the FSOG books, can't let go of them, remains obsessed with dominant rich men whose appetites combine romance with erotic discipline and the strong women who are moths to the flame: desperate for love, drawn to men who provide the right elixir: love, pain, pleasure, freedom, structure, support.

zoezelig@protonmail.com

Reviews[1]

Jon Zelig's Work:

Punishment Incorporated: The Full Trilogy
Protocols of the Sisterhood of the Gynarchy
Lose Your Wife in Three Easy Lessons: The Full Trilogy
Submitting to the Priestess Next Door

Four Reviews + Interview:
http://bibrary.blogspot.com/search?q=jon+zelig

Joy Zelig's Work:

Yes, No, Maybe: A Trilogy of Age Play Novellas
The Good Master: The Full Trilogy

Bram Zelig's Work:

Sister No More: An Erotic Vampire Romance

REV15AUG18

---

[1] Most available on Amazon and/or Goodreads.

Milton Keynes UK
Ingram Content Group UK Ltd.
UKHW011619270224
438561UK00006B/869